Lyndsey Main

Fairytales includes:

Cinderella

Goldilocks and the three bears

Hansel and Gretel

Little Red Riding Hood

The Three Little Pigs

Jack and the Beanstalk

Cinderella

Written by Susie Linn
Illustrated by Rosie Butcher

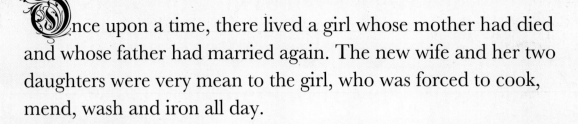

Once upon a time, there lived a girl whose mother had died and whose father had married again. The new wife and her two daughters were very mean to the girl, who was forced to cook, mend, wash and iron all day.

At night, the girl slept by the fire's glowing cinders,
so her ugly stepsisters called her ...

Cinderella.

One day, a letter came from the royal palace.
'The prince has invited us to a royal ball!'
shrieked one of the ugly stepsisters.

It was an invitation to all of the young ladies in the kingdom.
At the end of the night the prince was going to choose his bride!

The day of the ball soon arrived and the stepsisters were very excited. As they put the final touches to their outfits, Cinderella asked her stepmother what she might wear.

'You're NOT going to the ball!'
laughed her stepmother and stepsisters, cruelly.

Poor Cinderella felt upset,
so she ran outside and cried.
But just then ...

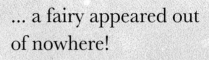
... a fairy appeared out of nowhere!

'**I'm your fairy godmother,**'
the fairy said, kindly.

With a flick of her magic wand, the fairy godmother transformed a nearby pumpkin into a beautiful carriage!

She changed two mice into horses!

Then she transformed a rat into a coachman and two lizards into footmen!

Finally, she turned Cinderella's scruffy dress into a beautiful ballgown, and birds fluttered down with a pair of glass slippers.

'*Enjoy the ball,*' said the fairy godmother.
'*But, make sure you're back home by midnight,
or the spell will be broken!*'

Cinderella thanked
her fairy godmother
and set off to the ball.

The palace looked magical in the moonlight and Cinderella was very excited. No one in the room recognised her, and everyone agreed that she was the most beautiful young lady at the ball!

The prince was enchanted by Cinderella's beauty and he danced with her all night. As the clock crept slowly towards midnight, Cinderella was having such a wonderful time that she forgot to leave!

DONGGG!

DONGGG!

DONGGG!

Suddenly, the clock struck twelve
and Cinderella remembered what her
fairy godmother had said.

Without a word, Cinderella fled and vanished into the night, leaving one of her glass slippers behind on the palace stairs.

The prince picked up the glass slipper
and called out to his servant,
**'Go and search the kingdom for the girl
whose foot fits this slipper! She is the girl I
wish to marry!'**

The weeks passed, and the prince's servant searched the whole kingdom, until only Cinderella and her ugly stepsisters were left.

The first ugly stepsister tried to squeeze and push her foot into the slipper, but no matter how hard she tried, her foot was too big.

Then the second ugly stepsister tried the slipper on, but her foot was too small.

'No luck here!'
exclaimed the prince's servant, and he turned to leave.

'**Wait!**' cried Cinderella's father. '**I have a daughter.**'

The stepmother and the ugly stepsisters looked at him in disbelief!

'**Her? She didn't go to the ball!**' shrieked Cinderella's stepmother.

'Hmm ...' thought the servant, looking at Cinderella. **'She seems familiar.'**

And with that, Cinderella slipped her foot into the glass slipper ... and it fitted perfectly!

Cinderella travelled nervously back to the palace,
but she did not need to worry. The prince recognised
her at once as the beautiful girl he had danced with.

'Will you marry me?' he asked Cinderella, taking her hand.
'Yes!' said Cinderella joyfully.

Cinderella and the prince were married
the very next day, and they lived happily ever after.

Goldilocks
and the three bears

Written by Nat Lambert
Illustrated by Rosie Butcher

Once upon a time, there were three bears;
Daddy Bear, Mummy Bear and Baby Bear.
Every morning the three bears all ate a bowl
of delicious porridge for breakfast.

One day, the porridge was too hot
so the three bears went
for a walk in the forest
so it would cool down.

Meanwhile, a little girl called Goldilocks was playing in the forest.
As she passed by the three bears' cottage, Goldilocks smelt
something delicious coming from inside.

Goldilocks was hungry so she peeped
through the window and saw three bowls
of porridge on the table.

'Mmmm, that porridge looks very tasty,'
she said, and crept into the cottage.

First, Goldilocks took a spoonful of porridge from the largest bowl.

'*Ouch!*' she squealed.
'*This porridge is far too hot!*'

Next, Goldilocks took a spoonful from the medium-sized bowl of porridge.

'*Yuck!*' she said, '*This porridge is far too cold!*'

Finally, Goldilocks took a spoonful from the smallest bowl of porridge.

'Mmm, this porridge is just right!'

So Goldilocks ate all of the porridge and even licked the bowl clean!

Now that Goldilocks wasn't hungry any more,
she began to explore the rest of the cottage.
First she wandered into the living room
where she saw three chairs.

First, Goldilocks sat down
on the largest chair.

**'Ouch! This chair is much
too hard!'** she grumbled.

Goldilocks then sat down on the
medium-sized chair.

**'Oh dear, this chair is
much too soft,'** she said.

Finally, Goldilocks sat down on the smallest chair.

'This chair is perfect!' smiled Goldilocks.

Goldilocks rocked back and forth until,
suddenly, there was a loud cracking noise
and the little chair collapsed beneath her!

Goldilocks tried to put the chair back together again, but it was well and truly broken. So, she quickly left the living room and went upstairs.

In the bedroom, Goldilocks
found three beds. She let out
a huge yawn, it had been a
busy day, and she was tired.

Goldilocks decided to
try the biggest bed.

'*Ouch! This bed is much too hard!*'
she complained.

Next, she tried the medium-sized bed.

'Oh dear! This bed is much too soft!' she said.

Finally, Goldilocks tried the smallest bed.

'This bed is perfect!' she sighed, as she snuggled down under the covers and fell fast asleep.

A little while later the three bears arrived
home from their walk.

They were glad to be home again
and were looking forward
to their breakfast.

'Who's been eating my porridge?'
growled Daddy Bear.

'Who's been eating my porridge?'
said Mummy Bear.

'And who's been eating my
porridge? It's all gone!'
cried Baby Bear.

The three puzzled, hungry bears went into the living room to sit down.

'Who's been sitting in my chair?'

growled Daddy Bear.

'Who's been sitting in my chair?'
cried Mummy Bear.

'And who's been sitting in my chair? It's broken!'
sobbed Baby Bear.

The three bears were very upset
that someone had been in the house,
so they went upstairs to look around.

**'Who's been sleeping
in my bed?'**

growled Daddy Bear.

**'Who's been sleeping
in my bed?'**

gasped Mummy Bear.

'And who's been sleeping in my bed ...
and is still there?'

whispered Baby Bear.

Just then, Goldilocks woke up and saw the three bears standing over her. She screamed loudly, leapt out of bed and ran as fast as she could, all the way home.

'I don't think she'll go into someone's house without being invited ever again!' laughed Daddy Bear.

'Now, let's make some more porridge!'

Hansel
and
Gretel

Retold by Karen Goddard
Illustrated by Ian Pointer

Once upon a time, there lived a

poor woodcutter named Jan and his two children Hansel and Gretel. Hansel was a brave and handsome boy with a mop of golden curls just like his father. His sister Gretel, with her long dark hair and deep brown eyes, had been blessed with the beauty of their mother.

The woodcutter's wife had died when the children were very young. Every time Jan gazed upon his daughter, he felt sad as he remembered his dear wife. Although Jan deeply missed Hansel and Gretel's mother, he was very lonely and longed for the company of a new wife.

Before long, the woodcutter decided to marry a widow from the village. She was a fearful woman with a fiery temper, but Jan hoped that she would make a good wife and mother.

She did not! The stepmother was cruel and unkind to Hansel and Gretel and

very soon the children realised that she would never love them as their real mother had done.

The woodcutter's wages did not stretch very far and, with four mouths to feed, the family were becoming poorer and poorer.

One night, Hansel and Gretel overheard their father and stepmother talking. Their stepmother had a wicked plan to make the family's money last longer. "Tomorrow you must take Hansel and Gretel deep into the forest, then leave them alone while you pretend to search for firewood," she said. "With those greedy children out of the way, there will be far more food for us." Jan tried to argue with his wife, but she insisted that he should carry out the evil scheme.

Hansel and Gretel couldn't believe their ears. How could their father betray them? The children, however, were a brave and clever pair and soon devised a plan of their own. They crept downstairs and searched the garden for as many small pebbles as they could find. Having filled their pockets with the tiny stones, they returned to their beds and waited anxiously until morning.

It was with a heavy heart that Jan led his two children into the forest the following day. Just as his wife had instructed, he told Hansel and Gretel to wait in a clearing whilst he collected logs for the fire. He then made his way home, leaving the children alone in the forest.

Unbeknown to their father, Hansel and Gretel had left a trail of pebbles from the cottage to the forest as they walked behind him. Once they realised their father really wasn't coming back for them, they followed the path of pebbles all the way home.

"Thank goodness you're safe," cried their father when he saw Hansel and Gretel at the door. He was pleased that the plan had failed. His wife, on the other hand, was furious. She glared at her husband and locked Hansel and Gretel in their bedroom without any supper.

Later that night, the children overheard the adults talking again. "Tomorrow, you must take Hansel and Gretel to the deepest, darkest part of the forest," said the stepmother, "and make sure that they never find their way back again."

Jan tried to protest. "How can you expect me to leave my own children in the forest to die?" he pleaded. The woodcutter's new wife was a cruel and heartless woman. "We can't afford to keep the children," she argued. "If we do, we are all doomed to die of starvation." Once again, the woodcutter reluctantly agreed to the plan.

The next day, Hansel and Gretel obediently followed their father into the forest. Since they had been locked in their room

the night before, they had not been able to collect any pebbles to drop on the path. Suddenly, Hansel had an idea. Instead of eating the crust of bread his father had given him, he began breaking it into crumbs and scattering it behind him as he walked. Gretel soon realised what her brother was doing and when Hansel had used up all of his bread, she continued the trail with her own piece.

When the time came for Jan to leave his children, he hugged them both with tears in his eyes. "Stay here and play whilst I go and collect logs," he said. "I shall return for you in two hours." With that, he walked off into the trees.

Hansel and Gretel were not down-hearted. They had found their way back home before and with the help of their secret trail, they were sure they could do so once again. When they looked for their breadcrumb trail, however, the children got a nasty surprise. It had completely disappeared! The hungry woodland birds had eaten every morsel of white crust – it seemed that this time Hansel and Gretel really were lost forever.

The children felt desperately sad and all alone. They sat down under a huge oak tree, huddled up close together and began to cry. Just then, Gretel noticed a beautiful bird with bright blue feathers and shining silver wings. She dried her eyes and nudged her brother.

"Hansel, look at that wonderful bird!" she exclaimed. "It seems to be calling to us." Sure enough, the bird was whistling a haunting tune and encouraging the children to follow it through the forest.

"Perhaps it knows the way home," said Hansel. "Let's go after it!"

The brother and sister held hands and followed the bird as it flitted from tree to tree. They walked for hours and became tired, thirsty and incredibly hungry. Just when they thought they could walk no further, the silver-winged bird led them to a clearing.

Hansel and Gretel could hardly believe their eyes – they were faced by a beautiful and magical sight.

In the clearing stood a cottage that was made entirely of gingerbread and sweets. Desperate for food, they ran up to the cottage and began licking the bricks, breaking off lumps of window ledge and nibbling the roof tiles.

Suddenly, an old woman appeared at the door. "You poor children," she said kindly, "you must be famished. Come inside and I'll prepare you a proper meal."

The children timidly followed the woman into the gingerbread cottage. True to her word, the sweet old lady provided Hansel and Gretel with a hearty supper of hot chicken soup and freshly baked bread. Then she offered them a bed for the night, which the tired children gratefully accepted.

The next morning, Hansel and Gretel felt happy and refreshed. They were sure that the mysterious and magical keeper of the gingerbread cottage would help them find their way back through the forest to their father's house. The woman who came to their room to wake them, however, was not the kindly, grey-haired old lady they had met the night before. In her place stood a hideous old witch with gnarled features and an evil glint in her eye.

The witch cackled hysterically, threw an apron at Gretel and told her to go down to the kitchen. Then she grabbed Hansel by the ear and dragged him downstairs too.

Gretel was told to get to work peeling potatoes, whilst her brother was thrown into a cage in the corner of the room. "This is what happens to greedy little children who come nosing around my cottage," screeched the witch.

She locked the door of the cage and hung the key on a hook high up on the kitchen wall.

Hansel and Gretel were shocked by the old woman's horrible transformation, but they were a quick-witted pair and knew that they could escape from the evil witch if only they could think of a way to distract her.

As Gretel took a closer look around the cottage, it became clear that she and her brother weren't the first unfortunate souls to stumble across the old witch's lair. Clothes, hats, purses and jewels belonging to the witch's previous victims were to be seen stashed under chairs, on shelves and in cupboards.

"If we could return home with all this money and jewellery, our worries would be over," thought Gretel.

The witch was an especially evil old woman. Not only did she steal the belongings of anyone who called at her cottage, but she took great delight in tempting the travellers inside, then boiling them up in her cauldron and eating them for her supper! Tender young boys were her particular favourite and she was looking forward to fattening up poor Hansel and then picking his bones clean

with her disgusting yellow teeth. The witch was also lazy, so it was left to Gretel to cook all the meals and clean the cottage every day.

The young girl had strict instructions to feed her brother well with thick broths, plenty of potatoes and lots of buttery cakes in order to plump him up ready for the pot.

Every morning, the witch would tell Hansel to poke his finger through the bars of the cage so that she could feel whether he was any fatter.

Having spent years eating the simple meals provided by his poor father, Hansel welcomed Gretel's daily diet of rich food. Try as he might, he just couldn't help devouring the delicious meals served up by his sister. Soon the boy's pale cheeks had become plump and rosy and the belt on his tattered trousers had become a little tighter. The children knew that if Hansel's fingers became too fat, the witch would eat him.

One day, whilst she was preparing soup, Gretel looked down at the chicken bones on the table. "Hansel," she whispered, "quickly take this bone and hide it in your pocket. When the witch asks to feel your finger, simply poke the bone through the bars of the cage instead. Her eyesight is so bad, she'll never notice the difference."

For a while, the plan seemed to work. Everyday, the witch inspected Hansel's bony finger and everyday she declared that he was still too skinny to be eaten. After three weeks of waiting, the witch finally lost her patience. "That's it," she cried, "I'm tired of waiting for you to get fatter. Tonight I will feast on roast leg of boy!" Then the witch ordered Gretel to heat up the huge oven.

Hansel and Gretel had been living in the cottage for quite a while. By now they knew that, as well as being cruel, lazy and very short-sighted, the witch was also rather stupid. The brother and sister were sure that they could out-wit the old woman one more time.

As the day wore on, the witch became increasingly excited about her evening meal. She flitted madly around the kitchen, gathering together ingredients and ordering Gretel to do this and to do that.

The witch was particularly worried about the temperature of the oven and kept asking Gretel to open the cast iron door to check that the stove was still alight.

"Stick your head inside girl," ordered the witch, "and make sure that the flame is still flickering." Hansel and Gretel looked at each other and smiled – they both knew that this could be the route to their escape.

"I'm afraid I can't reach to the back of the oven," replied Gretel sweetly, "could you help me please?" By now the witch was desperate for her dinner. She pushed Gretel aside angrily and grabbed the handle of the oven door.

"You stupid child," she screeched, "do I have to do everything myself?"

The witch opened the oven and poked

her head inside. At that moment, Gretel leapt into action. Quick as a flash, she pushed the witch headfirst into the hot oven. Then, the young girl slammed the heavy door shut. With the witch out of the way, Gretel could free her brother from his cage at last. She

grabbed a kitchen chair and climbed up to get the key from the hook.

"Well done, Gretel," said Hansel with a smile. "I couldn't have done any better myself."

The children were keen to escape from the gingerbread cottage as soon as possible, but they also knew that the witch's ill-gotten riches would come in very useful. They stuffed their pockets with as much money and jewellery as they could before leaving the witch's house forever.

"We may have escaped from the evil witch, but we still have to find our way home," Hansel reminded Gretel as they ran into the forest. Just then, the brother and sister heard a distant yet familiar voice calling their names.

"Hansel, Gretel, where are you?" It was their father, Jan. As soon as he left his children in the forest, he had regretted his terrible actions and had spent every day since searching the forest for Hansel and Gretel. His new wife, meanwhile, had grown tired of her husband's desperate attempts and was angry that he was earning even less money than before. She had stolen what little food the woodcutter had and returned to the village.

"I've found you at last," cried Jan when he saw his beautiful children running through the forest towards him. He clasped Hansel and Gretel to his chest and promised that he would never betray them again. "I would rather be a poor woodcutter than lose my dear Hansel and Gretel," he said.

"Father," cried Hansel, "we need never be poor again!" The two smiling children revealed their hoard of money and beautiful jewels. Jan was amazed and overjoyed. Not only had he found his children but, thanks to Hansel and Gretel, the family's money worries were at an end. With that, Jan and his two children made their way home to the woodcutter's little cottage where they lived happily ever after.

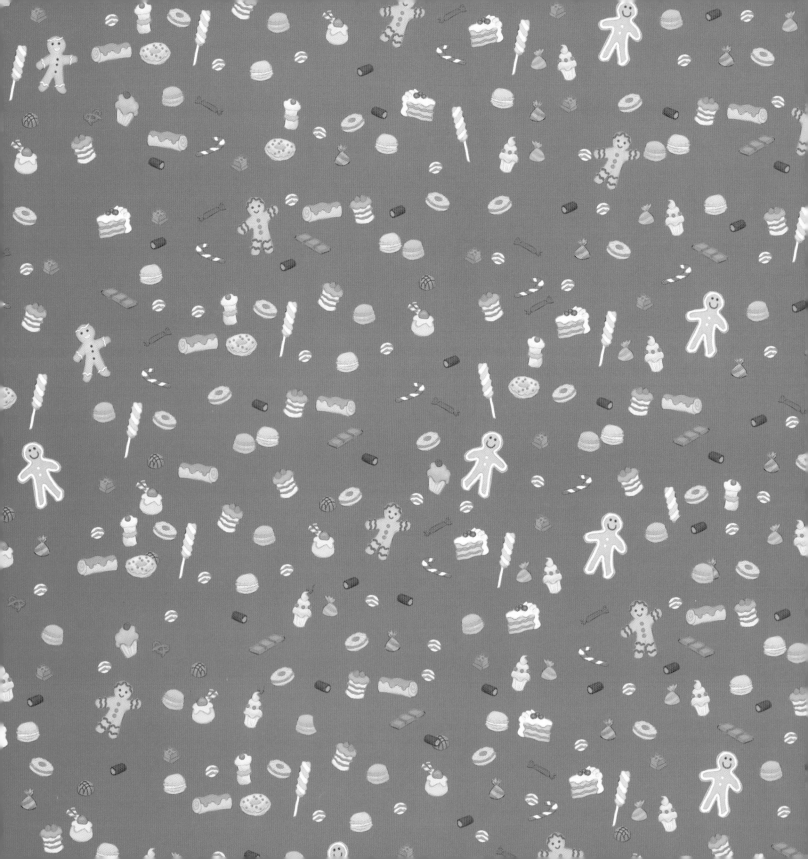

Little Red Riding Hood

Written by Nat Lambert
Illustrated by Rosie Butcher

Once upon a time, there was a girl called
Little Red Riding Hood, who lived at the edge of a
big, dark forest. Little Red Riding Hood had a
grandmother, who lived on her own in a cottage
on the other side of the forest.

One morning, Little Red Riding Hood set off to visit her grandmother for lunch, as she did every week.

Little Red Riding Hood skipped along the path through the forest, but soon she became tired and stopped to rest under a tree.

As she closed her eyes, Little Red Riding Hood
heard a voice behind her.

'Hello, little girl. Are you lost?'

'I'm not lost. I'm going to visit my grandmother, who lives in a cottage on the other side of the forest,' Little Red Riding Hood replied.

What Little Red Riding Hood didn't know was that she was talking to a big, bad wolf!

The big, bad wolf wanted to gobble up
Little Red Riding Hood right then,
but he decided he would race ahead
to her grandmother's cottage so
he could gobble them both up for lunch!

The wolf ran ahead until he reached Little Red Riding Hood's grandmother's cottage. He knocked on the door and listened.

'Who's there?' called a voice from inside.

'It's me, Little Red Riding Hood,' replied the wolf.

Knock, knock!

The wolf opened the door and before Little Red Riding Hood's grandmother could even scream, he gobbled her right up!

Quickly, the wolf put on her nightcap
and glasses and tucked himself up in bed.

When Little Red Riding Hood reached
her grandmother's cottage. She knocked
on the door and called out,

'Grandmother, it's me,
Little Red Riding Hood.'

'Come in,' said a voice from inside the cottage. So, Little Red Riding Hood opened the door and went inside.

Little Red Riding Hood thought that her grandmother looked a little strange, so she switched on a lamp near the bed.

'**Grandmother, what big eyes you have!**'
exclaimed Little Red Riding Hood.

'***All the better to see you with, my dear,***'
replied the wolf.

Little Red Riding Hood crept a little closer.

'Grandmother, what big ears you have!' gasped Little Red Riding Hood.

'All the better to hear you with, my dear,' replied the wolf.

Little Red Riding Hood crept right up to the bed.

'Grandmother, what big teeth you have!'
cried Little Red Riding Hood, as the light glinted off
the wolf's teeth.

'All the better to eat you with my dear!'
shouted the wolf, leaping out of bed.

Little Red Riding Hood screamed
and swung her basket as hard as she
could at the big, bad wolf.

The basket was very heavy and it knocked the wolf right over.

Just then, the door to the
cottage swung open and
Little Red Riding Hood's
father arrived, on his way
home from woodchopping.

Little Red Riding Hood
told her father all about
the big, bad wolf and how
he had eaten her
grandmother and tried
to eat her too!

Little Red Riding Hood's father took his enormous axe and very
carefully slit the wolf's tummy open …
and out popped Little Red Riding Hood's grandmother!

Little Red Riding Hood's grandmother was very happy
to be back and she agreed to come for tea at Little
Red Riding Hood's house. Little Red Riding
Hood, her grandmother and her father
walked out of the cottage and pulled
the door closed behind them.

'Good riddance, big, bad wolf,'
said Little Red Riding Hood.

The Three Little Pigs

Written by Nat Lambert
Illustrated by Rosie Butcher

Once upon a time, there were three little pigs
who lived with their mother. One day, it was time
for the little pigs to leave home and build their
own houses.

The little pigs couldn't wait to build their own houses so they set off happily on their journey.

As they walked along the road, the little pigs soon came across a man with a cart filled with straw.

'Ideal building material!'
said the first little pig.

So, after a day of hard work, the first little pig had built himself a fine house made of straw.

The two other little pigs looked
at his house and thought
that they could do better, so
they continued down the road.

A little further along the road, the two little pigs met a man with a cart loaded with sticks.

'Ideal building material!' said the second little pig.

So, after a few days of hard work, the second little pig had built himself a handsome house made of sticks.

The last little pig looked
at his house and thought
that he could do better.
So, he waved goodbye and continued further down the road.

Not much further along the road the
third little pig met a man
with a truck filled with bricks!

'This is exactly what I have been waiting for!
Ideal building material!' said the third little pig.

After weeks of hard
work, the third little pig
had built himself
a sturdy brick house.

One morning, a big, bad wolf was out for a walk when
he noticed the first little pig in his straw house.

'*Little pig, little pig, let me come in!*'
said the wolf.

'*Not by the hair on my chinny chin chin,*'
squeaked the first little pig.

'Then I'll huff, and I'll puff, and I'll blow your house down!' growled the wolf.

The wolf took a deep breath and blew down the house made of straw!

The first little pig ran as quickly as he could to the house made of sticks.

Following the first little pig,
the wolf arrived at the house
made of sticks.

'Little pigs, little pigs, let me come in!'
called the wolf.

'*Not by the hairs on our chinny chin chins,*'
squeaked the little pigs.

'*Then I'll huff, and I'll puff, and I'll blow your house down!*' growled the wolf.

The wolf took a deep breath and blew down the house made of sticks!

The two little pigs ran as quickly as they could to the brick house.

Again, the wolf followed the little pigs and reached the house made of bricks.

'Little pigs, little pigs, let me come in!'
shouted the wolf.

*'Not by the hairs on
our chinny chin chins,'*
squeaked the little pigs.

'Then I'll huff, and I'll puff, and I'll blow your house down!' growled the wolf.

But as much as he tried, the big, bad wolf couldn't blow down the house made of bricks.

But, the wolf wouldn't give up that easily! He climbed up to the top of the house and started to squeeze down the chimney.

Suddenly, the third little pig
had an idea …

Quickly, the three little pigs set a big pot
of boiling water over the fire …
just as the wolf squeezed down the chimney!

The wolf fell straight into the pot
of boiling water …
and that was the end of him!

The third little pig had outsmarted the big, bad wolf and built the strongest house.

He was a very clever
little pig indeed.

Jack
and the
Beanstalk

Retold by Gordon Volke

Illustrations by Ian Pointer

Once upon a time, there was a

widow who lived with her only son, Jack. This poor lady loved her boy very much, but he was lazy and selfish and wasted what little money they had on things for himself. In fact, it wasn't long before their savings had been completely used up and all they had left was one milk cow.

After a sleepless night, Jack's mother made a difficult decision. "You'll have to take the cow to market and sell her, Jack," she said. "Make sure you get a good price for her!"

On the way to the market, Jack met an old man. "Hey! Look at these!" called the stranger, showing Jack a handful of large beans.

"What about them?" asked Jack. "They look pretty ordinary to me!"

"Oh, no!" cried the old man. "They're magic beans. Would you like to buy them?"

Jack explained to the old man that he didn't have a penny to his name.

"What about the cow?" asked the stranger. "She must be worth a bit!"

"Of course!" exclaimed Jack. "I was on my way to market to sell her. I could swap her for your magic beans instead!"

When Jack got home, his mother was furious that he had swapped their cow for a handful of brown beans.

"You stupid boy!" she scolded. "Now we don't have any money at all. How are we going to live?"

"But these are magic beans, mum…" protested Jack.

"Nonsense!" shrieked his mother, snatching the beans out of his hand. She flung them as hard as she could out of the window.

"You've been tricked, Jack!" she shouted. "Those beans aren't magic. How could you have been so careless? Now we don't have any money to buy food and our cow is gone forever!"

That night, Jack went to bed feeling very miserable. He had no supper because the larder was empty and his mother was still very cross with him.

The following morning, Jack woke up expecting to see bright sunlight streaming through his window. Strangely, his room remained dark. Jack looked through the window and his jaw dropped in amazement.

Outside, in the garden, one
of the beans had grown into a
gigantic beanstalk, reaching right
up to the sky. Maybe the beans
were magic after all!

"MUM!" yelled Jack, rushing outside.
"Look at this!"

Jack had already started to climb the
beanstalk, when his mother came outside to find out what he was shouting about.

"Jack!" she called, anxiously. "Jack, come down!
The beanstalk might not be safe."

"It's as strong as a tree," Jack yelled back.

"But you don't know what you'll find
up there!" shouted his mother.

Jack wasn't listening. He was
already half-way up the beanstalk,
climbing as fast as he could.

As Jack's head poked through the clouds, he found himself in a strange country. There was grass as far as the eye could see and empty, treeless hills rose in the distance. Then, turning around, Jack was startled to see a house – and not just any house. This house was enormous!

Jack walked up to the house and knocked boldly on the front door. A giant woman opened the door and glared down at him.

"Go away!" she hissed, urgently. "My husband will be back soon. He doesn't like little boys, especially human ones!"

After his long, hard climb (and having gone to bed without any supper), Jack felt hungry and thirsty.

He wasn't afraid
of the giant and
begged the giant's
wife to let him
in and give him
something to eat
and drink. In the
end, she agreed.

Jack entered
the huge house
and looked around
in amazement.
All the rooms and
the furniture were twenty times bigger than in his own home.

Jack had just finished eating and drinking when the THUD, THUD, THUD
of approaching footsteps was heard outside.

"My husband's coming!" gasped the giant's wife.
"Quick! Hide in the empty oven."

The very next moment, the huge door burst open and in strode the most enormous man that Jack had ever seen!

"Fee, fi, fo, fum!" he chanted, and his voice echoed around the room. "I can smell a human one!"

Jack thought he would be discovered, but the giant's wife covered for him.

"No, dear," she said. "You can smell this bacon I'm frying for your supper. Now sit down and make yourself comfortable. I've done you three hundred rashers as usual."

Peeping out from his hiding place, Jack watched the giant gobble up his huge supper in a few quick mouthfuls.

After supper, the woman put a small brown hen in front of her husband. Jack was worried the giant would eat the hen too! Instead, the giant began gently stroking the bird

and cooing at her, like someone talking to a baby. Jack soon found out why. The giant's hen laid a golden egg. It rolled along the table, gleaming and sparkling in the light of the fire.

Jack quickly realised that this hen was the answer to all his problems. As soon as the giant dropped off to sleep and his wife was busy clearing up, the boy sneaked out of the oven, grabbed the hen and ran out of the house with it. He didn't stop running until he reached the top of the beanstalk. Then, without pausing for breath, he clambered down as fast as he could, clutching the hen tightly under one arm.

Jack's mother was waiting at the bottom of the beanstalk.

"Where have you been?" she cried. "I've been so worried about you!"

"Sorry," replied Jack, "but look – I've brought you this." He put the little brown hen down in front of his mother.

"Well, at least we'll have some eggs to eat tonight," said his mother with a sigh.

"Oh, we'll have more than that!" chuckled Jack, and just at that moment, the hen laid another glittering golden egg!

By selling their solid gold eggs, Jack and his mother soon became quite wealthy. They bought a whole herd of cows, so they always had milk and cheese, and they bought some ordinary hens to give them proper fresh eggs too.

Their larder was always full and they wore fine clothes. In fact, they had all they wanted and should have lived happily ever after.

Jack, however, had enjoyed his thrilling adventure in the strange land above the clouds so much that he wanted to take another look. Life was now comfortable, but dull, and the beanstalk still stood invitingly outside the kitchen window. One day, Jack kissed his mother goodbye and scrambled up through the giant leaves in search of new excitement. He carried a false beard in his backpack so that he wouldn't be recognised by the giant's wife.

Jack jumped from the top of the beanstalk and looked around him. Everything seemed the same as before, so he put on the false beard and headed for the giant's house. The giant's wife opened the door and, at first, refused to let him in.

"A while ago," she said, "I let a human boy into the house and he stole my husband's special hen. Never a day goes by without him grumbling about it!"

Jack, however, pleaded with the woman until she changed her mind and let him in for some food and drink. By the time the giant's heavy footsteps were heard approaching, Jack was safely hidden in a kitchen cupboard.

"Fee, fi, fo, fum." roared the giant. "I smell another human one."

"No you don't, dear," said his wife, quickly. "You can smell the roast beef I'm cooking for your supper."

The giant sat down with a grunt and gobbled down fifty joints of beef, five hundred roast potatoes and the biggest apple pies Jack had ever seen!

"Wife!" yelled the giant when he had finally finished eating, "bring me my money! I want to count it again."

The giant's favourite pastime after supper, now that his magic hen had gone, was to tip out his bag of silver coins and run them through his hands, making them sparkle in the firelight. Jack's eyes nearly popped out of his head when he saw how many coins the giant had saved!

Soon the giant's wife went up to bed, leaving her husband at the kitchen table. The giant carefully piled the coins into stacks, then counted each coin in every stack. Then he swept his enormous hand through the pile and started all over again. Just when Jack thought the giant would be awake all night, the giant poured the coins back into the bag.

Then, the giant gave a satisfied grunt and fell fast asleep in his comfy armchair. As soon as Jack heard the giant snoring, he silently sneaked out of the cupboard and picked up the bag of silver coins. It was terribly heavy and the coins chinked together when the bag moved, but the giant was sound asleep and Jack managed to get his stolen treasure out of the house without being discovered.

Jack slithered down the beanstalk where his mother was waiting.

"Promise me you'll never go up that beanstalk again," she said. "We have enough money now to last us for the rest of our lives!"

Three whole years passed before Jack began to feel restless again. He and his mother now had everything they wanted. They slept in soft, comfy beds, they both owned fine horses on which they went riding, they even enjoyed a holiday in a castle by the sea… but it was still not enough for Jack. Every day, he looked at the beanstalk outside his bedroom window and wondered what fantastic adventure awaited him if he climbed it again.

One summer morning, with his mother tugging at his clothes and pleading with him not to go, Jack climbed the beanstalk for the third time. On this occasion, he did not need a disguise. He had grown quite a lot in three years and was now a tall and handsome young man.

"Please go away!" said the giant's wife, opening the door of the huge house in the land above the clouds. "I get into terrible trouble every time I let a human enter. My husband has already lost his best hen and his bag of precious silver!"

Jack needed to use all his powers of persuasion to make the enormous woman change her mind. At last he succeeded and, following some refreshments, found

himself hiding in the larder. THUD, THUD, THUD! The giant's heavy footsteps were heard coming into the kitchen.

"Fee, fi, fo, fum!" growled the giant, "I can smell a human one!"

"Don't be silly, dear," called his wife. "That's the smell of the lamb stew that I'm cooking for your supper."

Now you would eat stew from a

plate, wouldn't you? Not this giant! He ate his stew from a bowl the size of a paddling pool, using a spoon the size of a grandfather clock and four hundred loaves of bread to wipe around the edges! When he had finished, the giant gave a burp that shook the house like an earthquake and then sat back, calling for his harp.

Jack watched in amazement as the giant's wife put a glittering gold harp beside her husband and it began to play beautiful music all by itself!

"That harp is all I need to finish my adventures with the giant," thought Jack, so he waited until the giant had been lulled to sleep by the enchanting music.

When Jack could hear the giant's snores and was sure that the giant's wife was out of the room, he leapt from his hiding place and grabbed the harp from the table. As he turned to run to the top of the beanstalk, to his horror, the harp seemed to come alive in his hands!

"Master, master!" called the magical instrument, sounding its strings all at once. "Help me, master! I'm being stolen by a horrible human!"

With a terrifying roar, the giant woke up and scrambled out of his chair.

He raced after Jack and his beautiful harp. At first, Jack thought he would get caught, but the giant was big and slow, and his tummy was very full of food. Tucking the harp under his arm and running faster than he had ever run in his life, Jack raced across the stony ground towards the beanstalk, keeping just ahead of the giant.

Scrambling down the beanstalk, Jack gasped as he realised that the giant had started to follow after him. By the time the boy reached the ground, the huge figure was already half-way down the beanstalk which was swaying under the weight.

"Mother, mother!" shouted Jack. "Fetch me the axe – as fast as you can!"

CHOP, CHOP, CHOP! Jack hacked away at the thick base of the beanstalk as fast as he could until there was an almighty CRASH. The massive beanstalk came tumbling to the ground.

Jack expected the giant to come tumbling down with the beanstalk, but with a roar of fury that echoed around the sky like thunder, the gigantic figure just managed to scramble back up to the top before he lost his grip.

Without the beanstalk there to tempt him, Jack never felt the need to go adventuring again. He married a beautiful girl, had two lovely children and looked after his mother as she grew older. Now he was a kind and thoughtful son, not the lazy and selfish one he had been before he climbed the beanstalk!